ISBN: 0-7172-8733-5

Manufactured in the United States of America.
A   B   C   D   1   2   3

DISNEY'S

TOY STORY

GROLIER
BOOK CLUB EDITION

Sheriff Woody faced the famous outlaw bank robber, Black Bart, as played by Mr. Potato Head!

"Reach for the sky, you rascal!" Sheriff Woody said.

Little Andy Davis aimed his two toys at each other. As always, Sheriff Woody won the fight.

Andy knocked over Mr. Potato Head and said, "Sorry, outlaw. Sheriff Woody was too fast for you. You lose."

Of all his toys, Andy loved Sheriff Woody the best.

Just then, Andy heard his mother calling him.

"Is it time for my birthday party?" he asked as he ran out of his room.

When Andy was gone, all his toys could walk and talk.

"Andy's birthday!" Woody said to himself. "This is terrible!"

Woody ran to Slinky Dog.

"Slink," he said quietly, "I've got bad news."

"BAD NEWS!" Slinky shouted.

"Shh!" Woody whispered. "Just get everyone together for a meeting."

Woody led the toys' meeting. "We'll all be moving to Andy's new house soon, so everybody should find a moving buddy," Woody told them. The toys nodded. They already knew about the move. Then Woody added quietly, "And Andy's birthday party is today." The toys panicked!

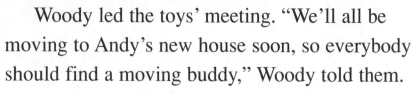

Later, Andy put the new toy on his bed. After he left, Woody and the other toys approached the stranger.

Suddenly the new toy jumped up. "My name is Buzz Lightyear, and I come to your planet in peace. My ship crash-landed here by mistake."

Rex the dinosaur got very excited. "Are you really here from outer space?"

Woody sighed. "Of course not. He's a toy, like us."

"Excuse me, but I think the word you're looking for is space ranger," Buzz told him. "I'm captain of the space fleet. And as soon as I fix my spaceship, I'll go back home."

All of the toys were impressed, except for Woody.

"I have special wings—I can fly," Buzz told him.

"No, you can't," Woody said.

"Can," said Buzz.

"Can't!" snapped Woody.

Buzz replied, "Yes, I can. And I can prove it."

Then Buzz leaped off the bed.

"To infinity and beyond!" he cried.

Buzz landed on a rubber ball . . . bounced onto a toy race-car track . . . slid down . . . slid up . . . then went flying through the air!

He landed right in front of Woody.

"Can," Buzz said smugly.

"That wasn't flying, that was falling with style," Woody scoffed.

But the other toys thought Buzz was great.

Suddenly the toys heard shouting. It was Sid, the boy next door. Sid liked to blow up his toys—and that's just what he was doing now!

The toys were glad they lived with Andy.

Andy loved his toys—especially his new one! He began playing with Buzz all the time. Woody became jealous.

One night, Andy was going to Pizza Planet for dinner. "You can only bring one toy," his mother told him.

Woody wanted Andy to bring him, not Buzz. So he tried to make Buzz fall behind Andy's dresser.

Woody aimed RC, a radio-controlled car, at Buzz. ZOOOOM!

Buzz jumped out of the way just in time!

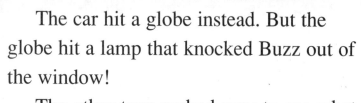

The car hit a globe instead. But the globe hit a lamp that knocked Buzz out of the window!

The other toys rushed over to see what had happened. They looked at RC.

The little car said, "Whirr, whirr."

The toys were surprised and angry. They
looked at Woody.

"You used RC to knock Buzz out of the
window!" Mr. Potato Head accused.

"No, no!" Woody cried. "I didn't mean to!"

The other toys didn't believe him. Woody
didn't know what to say. All the toys were
angry with him.

Bo Peep felt sad. She couldn't believe
Woody would do such a terrible thing.

Just then, Andy came into the room looking
for Buzz. But since Andy couldn't find his new
toy, he took Woody to the car instead.

Buzz was in the bushes nearby and saw
the car leaving. He quickly grabbed the car's
bumper.

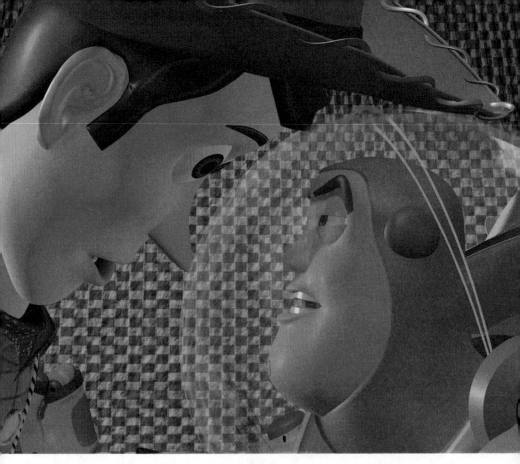

Andy's mother stopped for fuel. When Andy and his mother got out of the car, Buzz climbed in. Woody said, "I didn't mean to push you out of the window. Honest!"

Buzz didn't believe Woody. The two toys began to fight. They rolled out of the open car door. The car drove off without them! Luckily, Woody noticed a van from Pizza Planet. He and Buzz jumped aboard.

The van brought the toys to Pizza Planet.
The toys wanted to follow Andy's family
inside, but the door was guarded by robots.

"How are we going to get past the
guards?" wondered Woody.

Woody hid inside a big cup.

Buzz hid inside a burger box.

They sneaked past the robot guards.

Once they were inside, Woody spotted Andy.

But Buzz spotted a rocket ship! "Now I can go home!" he said.

He climbed inside the rocket.

The "rocket" was really a machine full of prizes. The prizes were little green alien toys.

"I come in peace," Buzz told the aliens.

Woody knew he had to rescue Buzz. So he climbed into the rocket, too.

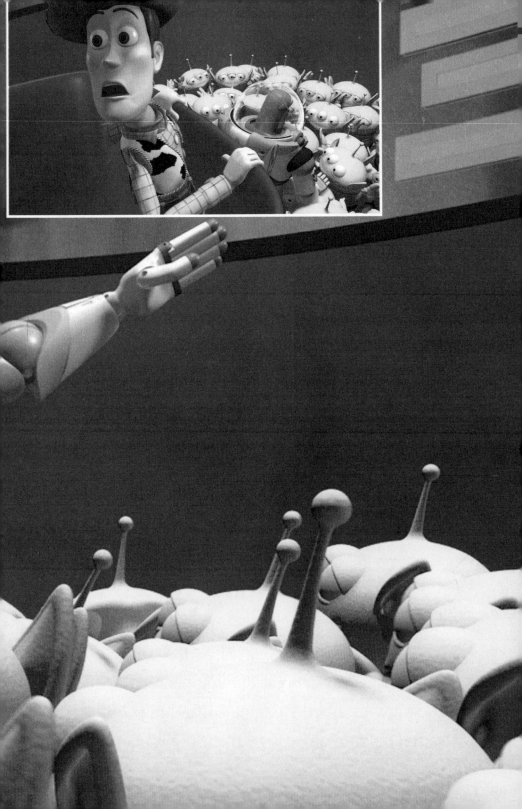

Suddenly a huge metal claw appeared.
The claw grabbed Buzz and lifted him up.
Someone wanted a prize from the rocket machine.

It was Sid!

Woody tried to save Buzz. Instead, Woody got picked up, too!

Sid laughed a nasty laugh. Now he had two new toys to destroy!

Sid took the toys home to his gloomy
room. After he left, Woody and Buzz looked
around. They saw something moving.

Buzz gasped. "What are those strange
creatures?"

Woody had never seen anything so horrible. Sid had ripped apart his toys and put them back together in weird ways.

The mutant toys moved closer and closer to Woody and Buzz. The two toys ran!

Woody and Buzz ran to different rooms. Then something even scarier happened to Buzz. He saw a TV commercial for a Buzz Lightyear toy!

Buzz said to himself, "That can't be right. I'm the *real* Buzz Lightyear! How can there be another one on TV?

"What if Woody is right? What if I am just a toy?"

Buzz had to prove he was the real space hero.
So he jumped off the top of the stairs.
Buzz spread his wings and . . . CRASH!

He hit the
ground so hard his
arm broke off.

Sid's sister found Buzz and brought him to her doll's tea party. Finally, Woody was able to sneak into her room.

"Hurry! Let's get out of here," Woody said.

Buzz replied sadly, "Why bother? I'm just a stupid toy. It doesn't matter who plays with me."

As they went back to Sid's room to try to escape, Woody tried to convince Buzz that being Andy's toy was just as important as being a space ranger.

Suddenly the mutant toys surrounded Buzz. To Woody's surprise, they fixed Buzz's broken arm.

Just then, Sid turned up. He taped a rocket to Buzz. He was going to blow him up the next morning.

Woody had to save Buzz. But he couldn't
do it alone. He bravely approached Sid's
mutant toys. They were friendly! And they
agreed to help.

The next morning the mutant toys followed
Woody to Sid's backyard.

"Reach for the sky!" Woody shouted at Sid.
Sid turned around. He looked at Woody in
shock. How could a toy
talk by itself?

"We toys don't like being blown up. We don't like to be smashed or ripped apart," Woody told Sid.

The boy gasped. He saw dozens of toys heading straight for him.

Woody said, "You'd better take good care of your toys. If you don't, we'll find out, Sid!"

The nasty boy screamed and ran to his room. He would never blow up a toy again.

Woody and the other toys cheered.

Suddenly Woody saw the moving van
in front of Andy's house. He and Buzz had to
get on it!

They raced out of the yard with Sid's
vicious dog chasing them.

Buzz rescued Woody from the dog, but he
was left behind as the moving van pulled
away. Woody had to help his friend.

Inside the van, Woody opened the box with the toys and got RC. Then he pushed RC down the van's ramp.

The other toys didn't understand. They thought Woody was trying to get rid of RC, too. So they pushed him off the van.

The van sped away.

Buzz and Woody hopped on the speeding car.

They raced to the van—and almost made it!

Unfortunately, RC's batteries died.

Woody cried, "Oh no! Now we'll
never catch up with the van."

But then he got another idea. Woody lit the rocket that was taped to Buzz.

WHOOSHH!

As RC sped up the van's ramp, Buzz spread his wings and . . . he and Woody were flying!

Woody and Buzz flew right into the car!

Andy was so happy. He had thought Woody and Buzz were lost. But they were right there in the car! Andy hugged his toys.

Buzz realized that Andy loved him. Now he knew what it meant to be a toy. It was even better than being a space hero.

Woody, Buzz, and all the toys were happy in Andy's new home. Soon it was Christmas. The toys were nervous. What if Andy got new and better toys?

The toy soldiers went to watch Andy and his sister open their gifts.

"Don't worry," Bo Peep said to Woody. "Andy will always love you." She kissed Woody's cheek.

Woody told Buzz, "We have nothing to worry about. Andy couldn't possibly get anything worse than you."

Then the toy soldiers made their report: Andy got a puppy!

"Uh-oh!"